# The Chick
# and the Duckling

Translated from the Russian of V. Suteyev

by Mirra Ginsburg
Pictures by Jose Aruego & Ariane Dewey

Aladdin Paperbacks

First Aladdin Paperbacks edition 1988

Text copyright © 1972 by Mirra Ginsburg
Illustrations copyright © 1972 by Jose Aruego

Aladdin Paperbacks
An imprint of Simon & Schuster Children's Publishing Division
1230 Avenue of the Americas
New York, NY 10020

Printed in Hong Kong
20   19   18   17   16

to Libby

A Duckling came out
of the shell.

"I am out!" he said.

"Me too," said the Chick.

"I am taking a walk,"
said the Duckling.

"Me too,"
said the Chick.

"I am digging a hole,"
said the Duckling.

"Me too,"
said the Chick.

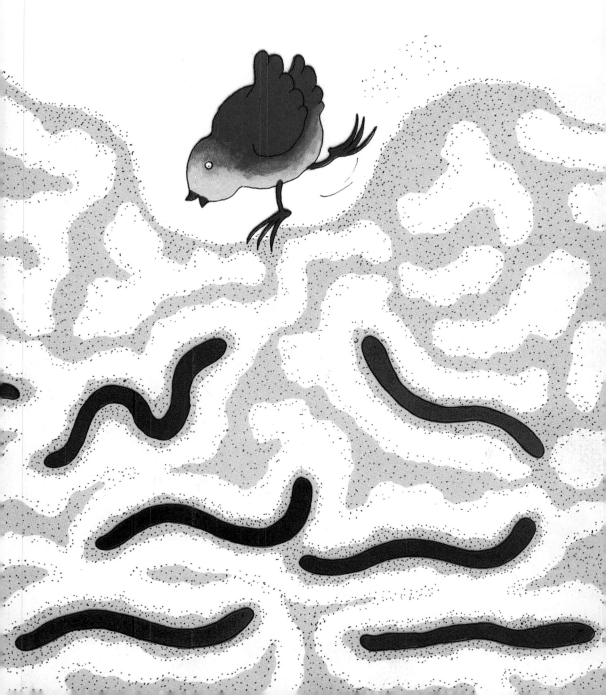

"I found a worm,"
said the Duckling.

"Me too,"
said the Chick.

"I caught
a butterfly,"
said the
Duckling.

"Me too,"
said the Chick.

"I am going for a swim," said the Duckling.

"Me too,"
said the Chick.

"I am swimming,"
said the Duckling.

"Me too!"
cried the Chick.

# The Duckling pulled the Chick out.

"I'm going for another swim," said the Duckling.

"Not me,"
said the Chick.